All Through the Night

All Through the Night

Traditional Lyrics by
Sir Harold Boulton

Illustrated by
Gary and Steve Fasen

Abingdon Press
Nashville

All Through the Night

Produced for Abingdon Press by Carnival Press, Inc. © 1988.

ISBN 0-687-01015-2

Typestyle: Goudy Oldstyle, 30pt
Printed in Hong Kong on low-acid paper
1 2 3 4 5 6 7 8 9 10

We dedicate this to the children.

Sleep my child and peace attend thee,
All through the night;

Guardian angels God will send thee,
All through the night;

Soft the drowsy hours are creeping,

Hill and vale in slumber sleeping;

I my loving vigil keeping,
All through the night.

While the moon her watch is keeping,

All through the night;

While the weary world is sleeping,
All through the night;

O'er thy spirit gently stealing,
Visions of delight revealing;

HAPPY BIRTHDAY

Breathes a pure and holy feeling,

All through the night.

All Through the Night

All Through the Night, which is based on a traditional Welsh folk song, has become a popular lullaby all over the world.

The original melody was arranged for the violin and cello in 1803 by Franz Josef Haydn (1732-1809). Haydn, an Austrian composer, rewrote a great number of Scottish, Irish, and Welsh folk songs in his later musical career. His arrangement of the Welsh folk song was titled *Ar Hyd y Nos (The Live Long Night).*

In 1884 Sir Harold Edwin Boulton (1859-1935), a Scottish lyricist and prose writer, rewrote the words of the original Welsh folk song. He combined his words with the music of *Ar Hyd y Nos* to create the lullaby *All Through the Night.*